SILENCE IS SILVER

Silence is Silver
A Shadowbinders Story
Copyright 2024 by Andrew Watson
First Edition: June 2024
ISBN: 978-1-7393400-2-5 (Hardback)
ISBN: 978-1-7393400-3-2 (Paperback)

Cover Design by Chris Nazgul
Map by Joshua Hoskins
Edited by Sarah Chorn

To Lewis

There is strength in blood

Books by
Andrew Watson

The Shadowbinders Trilogy
Harbinger of Justice
The Black Mantle

Novellas
Silence is Silver

SILENCE IS SILVER

A Shadowbinders Story

Andrew Watson

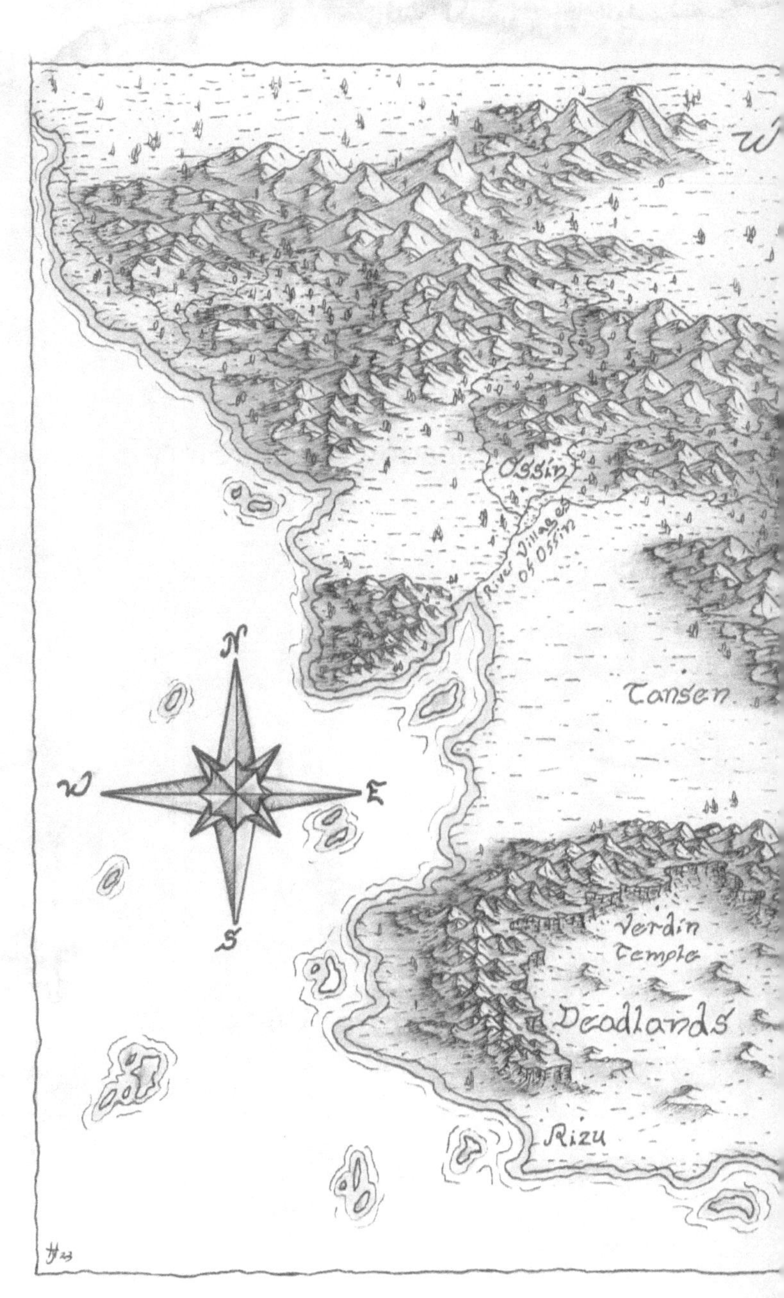

N
W
E
S
Ossin
River Village of Ossin
Tansen
Verdin
Temple
Deadlands
Rizu

ands
Gailion
Asuriya
Karbari
Yonfar
Celabar
Dock
Town
TARRIS

1

Silencers of Thought

"Pain is a lie. Told to us by weakness."

- Urdahl Proverb

Pain isn't a constant. It ebbs and flows like the sand dunes. Insurmountable peaks pass in a breeze. Stone erodes to dust. Pain is the body's defence against discomfort. But if one can quiet their mind, they can achieve anything. The Urdahl are called the Silencers of Thought for they have mastered the practice.

Bas heard more than felt the hollow thud of a fist cracking against his chest. He did not pull away from the blossoming pain but focused on it, feeling the rise and fall of heat.

Crack.

Feeling it sharpen and dull.

Crack.

Warm and cool.

Crack.

Spread and ease.

Crack.

Pain is temporary. Nothing lasts and everything fades.

It was the first lesson of the Urdahl. Knowing pain, under-standing it will come and go like the sandstorms, lets one relax into it. It will ease. It will pass. And it will come again.

Another crack.

Bas kept his eyes closed so he could focus on the sensations filling his body; the explosion of pain and how it pulsed and faded, the contrasting breeze being carried through the tunnels of the Settlement and how it caressed his bald scalp, making it prickle in the cool.

He glanced up to see two of his Urdahl siblings taking turns punching his torso. Coarse rope ripped through the skin on his wrists as Bas hung suspended by a rock. He swayed with each impact.

They were in a huge dome-shaped cavern. A crack of sunlight lined the middle of the space with a burning fissure of heat. Bas hung in the shade but other Urdahl sparred in the light. Using the lines of the Sun Eye's gaze as the edges of their ever-shifting arena.

Eventually, Bas' siblings stopped battering him and he let his head fall to his chest as he took deep breaths.

"And you see," Rfan said, her loose, tan robe whipping in the wind. The billowing breeze did little to hide her toned, muscular form. With a sharp nose and chiselled jawline, she resembled a stone carving of a human. "You will learn to quiet the child that demands you pull away from pain."

Bas' other sibling, Mei, loosed the rope letting Bas drop to the sand. The ground was rough and sharp, cutting into his skin and bringing no respite from the rope. Bas' muscles spasmed as he steadied his breathing.

"Showing little pain can dissuade your enemy. It can make you look strong even if you don't feel it," Rfan said.

Before them, twenty-two children sat cross legged in the sand watching the display. They were of the 712th year, making them ten years old. Of age to begin the iron bone training, where one would be hit over and over to strengthen their body. Then they would move onto iron fist training where they would learn to direct that power by punching stone until their knuckles bled.

Bas leant against the rock as Rfan continued to talk with the 712th siblings. He kept his mind clear allowing the pain to fade.

"You did well," Mei said.

Bas nodded suppressing a groan as his chest throbbed. Even silhouetted by the light, Mei's soft features contrasted that of Rfan's, her brown hair singed by sunlight. Mei held out a hand and yanked Bas to his feet.

Ever inquisitive and studious, Mei knew the Urdahl practices by heart. And yet she never fell behind on the physical training despite her scholarly nature. Bas always respected her for that.

It was of the Urdahl to not get too connected to those around them. Even those within their sibling year. But among their siblings, Mei was the one he sat with in the feast cavern and who he sparred with during training.

"We begin from the bottom and work up," Rfan was saying to the children. "Can anyone guess where we will start?"

Several of the children raised their hands. Rfan picked the fastest.

"The fire walk?" the child asked.

Some of the children flinched at the mention of the training practice. Rfan would have noticed and they would pay for showing their fear with extra time upon the fire walk.

"Yes," Rfan said. "That is correct. Now come."

The children lined up as Rfan walked over to Bas and Mei.

"Eri is missing. Bas, you will go find him. Mei, come with me," Rfan said.

While all in their year were equals, it was customary to follow the word of the strong and there was no doubting Rfan was the strongest of the 700th year siblings. And she made sure the others knew it.

Bas bowed as Rfan and Mei led the children through a tunnel in the rock wall. Bas then took off in the opposite direction, passing through the tunnels of the Settlement. The Urdahl had many burrows throughout the desert all connected through a tunnelling system deep beneath the sand. But only one section was called the Settlement. It was where those in training went when they came of age.

The tunnels around the Settlement were some of the largest. Several Urdahl could walk abreast here but the further one got from the main settlements the narrower the tunnels became. Bas bowed in reverence to those he passed. The firelight of the sconces flickered and shook playing with the breeze. The tunnels had been designed by the ancients to capture the gales and send them flowing through the settlements to keep them cool in the dry heat of the desert.

The elders claimed the wind carried whispers of the past and the future, and that one could hear their fate if their soul was still. The draught carried at Bas' back and battered against his hearing, dulling his senses and making him feel light. He hadn't ever caught a word on the wind but he always calmed his mind and strained his hearing whenever he wandered the tunnels.

Turning out of the main tunnels, Bas headed for the 712th year's chambers. Alcoves were cut into the cavern's wall creating over a hundred nooks for the 712th year siblings to sleep in and a crack in the rock above let in the Sun Eye's pale light.

An elderly woman approached Bas carrying a pile of clothing. Maut Tenl had short-cropped grey hair and a pronounced nose. She was the mother of the 712th year of siblings. Of course, she was not of their blood. Bas had read of the Tarrisian people who roamed the cities upon the desert sand. They were strange and their world seemed so far away.

Blood parents cared for their children even if they were not suited to such tasks. Whereas with the Urdahl, every child born within a year was given to a maut, which meant mother in the old tongue. It was much like the villages in the desert that would have a maut, who cared for the people of the village.

Urdahl never learnt their true parentage for it was meaningless. Their maut was trained to be the best mother a year of children could hope for. They taught them the skills they needed to know to survive in the world.

Bas bowed. "Maut Tenl, sorry to disturb you but have you seen Eri? He wasn't at training this morning."

Tenl took a breath. "I warned him and yet his head remains in the sky burning under the Sun Eye's gaze. He set out to read early this morning."

"I will find him."

"Thank you, Bas," Maut Tenl said and sidled past him muttering under her breath.

If Eri wasn't here, there was only one other place he would be. This wasn't the first time the distractible boy missed training, much to the frustration of Maut Tenl and the elders. Bas spun on his heels and took to the tunnels.

The tunnels narrowed as Bas wound his way further from the Settlement to the Wayup cavern. The fresh earthy scent of the desert poured into the wide cavern from the desert above. It was one of the main entrances into the Settlement. A sandfall hissed at the back of the cavern. A perpetual flow of sand.

"Eri! You have missed the start to your iron training," Bas called. His voice echoed through the empty space.

The clomp of a book being shut was his response and the young boy's head popped out of a ridge in the rock wall.

"Is Rfan teaching?" Eri asked.

Bas nodded and noted the flicker of concern that quirked the boy's face. He jumped up and clambered down from his perch on the wall with ease.

"I was lost in the story," Eri said, his blonde hair bobbing as he ran over. Bas held out his hand and Eri handed him the book. The slim leather volume was from the library.

"Voice of the People," Bas read.

"Yes. It's a story of a great hero," Eri said, excitement lining his tone. No matter how many times Maut Tenl told him to contain his emotions, Eri couldn't when talking about stories. His blue eyes gleamed as he spoke. "He starts on the streets of Yontar with his sister until she is kidnapped by a demon who plans to rule the world. So he sets off to save her and to kill the demon."

"You can't miss the start of training, Eri," Bas said. "Rfan will have you walking the fire walk twice as much as your siblings now."

Eri looked at his feet, kicking a rock. Bas wanted to shake the boy and warn him of all that comes to those who do not take to the Urdahl ways. Discipline is a nail that can only be hammered into one's bones.

Bas sighed.

"Well?" Bas asked.

The boy cocked his head.

"Did he save his sister at the end of the story?" Bas asked.

"Of course." Eri leapt, hand outstretched like he was pointing a sword. *"Pain is inevitable but that inevitability is not a right to inflict it upon others!"* Eri shouted in his best hero voice.

After a moment, his hand fell to his side and a smile tugged at the side of his mouth. "He meets many people in his travels that join him and together they fight against the demon who took his sister. They go through so much but they're stronger for it."

Bas slipped the tome under his arm. "This hero must have spent a lot of time training to accomplish such feats."

The smile on Eri's face faded.

"Come on."

They passed back out into the wind tunnels heading for the fire walk. Eri walked a step behind Bas to show deference.

"Why do you always read in the Wayup cavern?" Bas asked. He had always wondered why the boy went there to read instead of in the temple where the books were kept.

"I like to look out across the desert," Eri said. "It makes me think of what could be out there. It makes me think maybe I could go out and adventure like in the stories. Have you ever been outside the Settlement?"

Bas nodded.

"What was it like?" Eri asked.

They came to the front of the Temple of Ma-nivi, deity of knowledge. Once it had sat above the sands but with time the desert took it, and now buried, the Urdahl had claimed it. The ancient Urdahls, the first of the burrowing people, had dug it out and it had become a centre of the Settlement, where they kept their knowledge. Great steps led up to a row of pillars depicting Ma-nivi. The deity was owl-like with large round eyes and long outstretched wings that wrapped around the pillars. Beyond that, the entrance into the temple stood as a gaping hole in the rock three times the height of the tallest Urdahl.

"Loud," Bas said. They came to a stop at the base of the steps. The rest of Tarris were an undisciplined people and their ways confused Bas. It lacked structure and sense of togetherness. "I went to Yontar with Elder Wyan to collect some supplies."

"I want to be a wandering Urdahl and see Yontar," Eri said.

Bas suppressed a surge of alarm and grabbed Eri's shoulder, looking about to ensure no one overheard him. "Never say such things."

Eri dipped his head. "Sorry. I just meant that I want to see Tarris."

"A wandering Urdahl is one abandoned by the elders and the Settlement. They are no more Urdahl than those in the city. Never speak of them."

If anyone were to hear the boy talk like that, he would be punished. Bas knew he should report what Eri had said but with his wandering mind the mauts were already concerned for the boy's purpose. The Urdahl were a secret people and did not take kindly to those who wanted to leave the Settlement.

Two elders walked by looking suspiciously at the two of them. Bas and Eri bowed and they matched the gesture. Once they had passed, Bas patted the boy's shoulder. "There are ways to see the world while remaining Urdahl."

Eri's head snapped up, eyes wide. "How?"

"Those with purpose and a mission may leave the Settlement and see Tarris," Bas said. "Once you have become a full-fledged Urdahl you may be given tasks which lead you to far off lands."

Eri's back straightened and a grin spread across his face. Bas couldn't help but warm to the boy's elation.

"But only the best of us may be given such freedoms. You must work for it," Bas said.

"I will." Eri nodded.

"To become like the heroes in these books," Bas tapped on the book, "You need to focus on your training. Become still of mind."

The boy nodded again.

"Good. Now run along to the fire walk and I will return this book," Bas said.

Eri bowed and held it like one might to an elder. "Thank you, Bas."

And with that the boy ran into the wind tunnels. Eri was undisciplined and erratic. He still had the mind of a child that fled from pain and sought out the new and exciting but discipline could be learned. The boy had a good heart and soul and that was something that could not be learned. It either was or wasn't.

Bas headed up the steps and into the temple.

The Great Fire roared in the middle of the ruins within the cavern. A village, its name lost to the ages, was now little more than a skeleton dragged into the sand, made up of half-standing homes and walls that rose no further than Bas' ankles. It was late in the evening and the many cooks sat atop the ruins over the Great Fire cooking the nightly meal. A line of Urdahl snaked through the ruins to the fire where mauts handed out platters of cooked meats and hard breads.

The alluring scent pulled on Bas as he collected his plate with a bow and wandered through the feast cavern. Smaller fire pits burned around the space. Smoke billowed up to the high ceiling of the cavern where tube-like holes branched out and fed the smoke out to the desert above.

Bas found Mei at her usual spot and sat with her in companionable silence as they ate their meals. Other 700th year siblings gathered round the fire pit as many other year siblings joined them too.

Tearing into his food, Bas closed his eyes, relishing the soft meat. Murmurs of conversation hummed under the roar of the Great Fire and groans of the metal poles turning the meat above it.

The feast cavern was painted red in the firelight. Stone walls acted as benches around what was once a home but now a place for their evening meal. Bas stared into the flames as he ate. His mind roaming elsewhere.

"Something is on your mind," Mei said, placing her bowl on the ground at her feet. Bas never understood how she could always see through his placid exterior. His chewing slowed as she met his gaze.

It wasn't of the Urdahl to lie but he wasn't sure how much of his conversation with Eri he wanted to share.

"Have you ever thought about going on errands outside the Settlement?" Bas asked.

The slight twinge in Mei's face was as close to a questioning look one would get from an Urdahl.

"Sometimes," Mei said. "I'm sure there is a lot to learn from the rest of Tarris. But I'm not sure I need to. There is enough here in the Settlement for me to learn something every day and not make a dent in our knowledge as a people."

"Sure." Bas hesitated. He thought about Eri and his dream of being a hero that helped people. "What about helping other Tarrisians?"

Mei stared at him.

Bas placed his bowl at his feet and sat closer to Mei. "We train to become Urdahl and that is the reward. I understand that. But what if we could help others, too? We could use our training to protect those who need it."

Mei continued to stare at him. "You've been spending too long with that Eri boy and his stories of heroes."

Turning back to the flames, Bas felt a pit in his stomach. She was right. Heroes did not exist outside of stories. He knew that. But spending time with Eri made him wish such people existed.

"One must stand back and see what is of the Urdahl. Be that their own death or the death of the innocent," Mei recited the proverb in her singsong way.

"You're right. It was a foolish thought," Bas said.

They were a secretive people. Errands above the sands were in companies of three to ensure that none of their ways were discovered. These heroes in Eri's stories were but a child's wandering fancy. They did not have to live with the harsh realities of the world. The carefully curated tales revealed little of the true complexities of life.

It was only after the Urdahl had time to finish their meals did Elder Niru step out from high in the ruins. The Urdahl silenced at the sight, all glancing at their leader. The decrepit building acted as a sort of dais for the elder to look upon his people.

Niru was the oldest and wisest of the elders. Time had bent his back and strained his senses but the man still trained every day and remained strong and settled. He was unadorned compared to the monarchs and nobles of the cities. He did not need garish clothing to show his position. Instead, he wore what most of the Urdahl wore: baggy black breaches and a light tan over shirt that hung loosely to his frame. Long white hair fell resplendent and seemingly glowing in the firelight.

"Blessed Urdahl, it is the turning season," Elder Niru said. His voice carried in the quiet. The echoing boom added strength to his words. "With the turning season, some will begin the next stage of their training. Others will be tested. But none will complete their training. As like Ova the World Turner, there is no end to our watch. An Urdahl must remain sharp and unflinching. A sword can only remain sharp should it be attended to regularly.

"As a year of siblings moves to the next stage of their training they continue a practice that will last them a lifetime. A practice to strengthen muscle and mind. But the turning season is also a time to celebrate. One must not undervalue the passage of time. And one must not undervalue their efforts of surviving the storms and serenity that come with it.

"All siblings have already begun their new training. And soon the 700th year siblings will begin their testing for this turning season."

Bas sat up straighter.

"The Seeing Bowl is being prepared for tomorrow morning. And the Passage of the High Pass will follow the day after," Elder Niru said. Some of the younger year siblings whispered amongst themselves before being scolded by their mauts. The testing was what all Urdahl trained for. It was what turned them into fully-fledged Urdahl. And now it was Bas' years' turn.

"I wish you all the best of luck and I hope to see you all at the celebratory feast in three nights.

"May you find the still in the storm."

With that, Elder Niru turned and disappeared into the remnants of the building.

Rfan cleared her throat from across their fire pit. "The time to prove ourselves has come," Rfan said, hands outstretched to her siblings. "Let's show that we are of the Urdahl."

The 700th year siblings stomped their feet and others battered their chests. Urdahl from all around the cavern looked their way. The hairs on the back of Bas' neck prickled.

The turning season had begun.

2

The Seeing Bowl

"Strength to help others begins with the strength to help oneself."

- Urdahl Proverb

Bas swore he could *smell* water. He sat perched on a rocky escarpment in a meditative position, eyes closed against the morning light. Today he would sip from the Seeing Bowl. He would look into the space between spaces and see… something. None of the Urdahl ever spoke of what they saw. It was forbidden. But tomes spoke of the many visions of the bowl. Some told of a past from centuries ago, others were shown the future. And some were said to have been given prophecies from deities.

But it always spoke of the Urdahl finding purpose in the sight. It was unique to the individual Urdahl and therefore it must be held tight and never revealed to another.

Sweat trickled down Bas' brow. He felt the urge to brush it away, to itch where it tracked through the dust and sand upon his face. He let the sensation pass. Part of the Seeing Bowl ritual was that one must not have anything to drink on the day. While Bas had trained to go without water in the desert for some time since he was a child, today it was difficult. The sweat beading upon his skin called to him and the Sun Eye's heat was unrelenting in its burning watch. His mind scattered in his meditation. Thoughts rose and refused to be discarded.

To sip from the Seeing Bowl was to be given purpose from the Gods. To survive the Passage of the High Pass was to prove one's strength of muscle and mind. It was to make one of the Urdahl. It was what Bas had trained for his entire life.

Why then did his mind whisper inescapable words of despair?

Why then did a voice tell Bas he would fail? It was always there and berated him for his mistakes. It told him he was foolish to believe he could become a full Urdahl.

His thoughts fell to Eri. He was young and his mind wandered like Bas' once did. Bas felt a connection with the boy and it was only now he realized why. He reminded Bas of himself at that age. He too had loved stories of heroes that travelled to far off lands. But Bas hadn't picked up a book in years. When had that love faded?

Bas exhaled and opened his eyes. The desert stretched golden towards the red horizon. A beam of sunlight shone through a hole in one of the rocky peaks landing between two markings on the stone wall. Urdahl used the moving Sun Eye's gaze to mark times passing. The light was perfectly aligned with the turning season.

He slid a hand into his bag and pulled out the book Eri had been reading. He was going to return it. But it was best to see what Eri was filling his head with first. Bas opened the book and started reading.

Soon he was lost in the story. All thought of water and worry washed away beneath a tale of heroism and struggle. Before he knew it, he had worked his way through most of the book. The world between the pages was one he didn't recognise. The Urdahl spoke of struggle and pain as inevitable, while the book followed characters who strove to create a place free of strife. As if it could be killed like a beast.

That was wrong.

Pain came as sure as night. Without it, daylight would dull and fade into the ever ways of the world. There was no softness without the sharp sting of the rocks. There was no ease without the burden of a full pack.

There was no strength without suffering.

Still it was nice to pretend for a time.

The Sun Eye had marched across the sky. Bas' eyes sharpened. He had been reading for longer than he thought.

It was time.

Pressing through the wind tunnels, Urdahl nodded in passing. They all knew where the 700th year siblings were headed and what awaited them. Bas steadied his mind and let it clear. While the story was a lie one lived in, Bas couldn't deny the profound effect it had on settling his wandering mind.

Behind one of the temples, a crack in the rock wall was covered by a red tarp. A curling insignia that looked to be blood sloshing in a bowl was stitched into the fabric. Bas pushed it aside and ducked through the gap.

The Settlement had cracks letting sunlight fill the spaces and braziers lined most walls but this passage was thick in shadow. Bas continued through the dark unphased. Ahead, low chanting sounded as the edges of the tunnel took shape in a bleeding red.

The Red Chamber.

A cavern opened before Bas. It was a small chamber with a roaring fire in the centre. More than half of his 700th year siblings were already seated crossed legged around the flames.

Bas sat near the fire. Elder Urdahl stood against the cavern walls chanting quietly. The chanting wasn't in a language Bas knew and the words sounded strange to his ears. Somehow soft and sharp at the same time. Impossible and unusual sounds. Almost like they were not coming from the lips of humans.

The elders wore red robes that Bas had never seen before. The heavyset robes were hooded and shrouded the elders' faces in shadow and the same insignia that had been at the tarp was stitched onto their breast.

The rest of the 700th year siblings arrived one by one. Bas nodded to Mei as she stepped into the chamber. She returned the gesture but no words passed between them or anyone. The chanting reverberated around the small cavern. It grew louder once they had all seated around the fire.

One of the red-robed elders exited under a tarp on the far

wall and returned with the Seeing Bowl.

It was a simple thing. Bas had expected an ornate bowl of gold and silver but this was deep black and unadorned. Bas' heart beat faster. Despite being little more than a normal bowl something in his soul trembled as it drew closer.

The elder walked to the fire, where a metal frame held a pot. He tipped the bowl towards it letting the goopy red blood drip into the pot. It sizzled and spat then a sudden rush of red smoke plumed from the pot filling the cavern. The unmoving elders chanted louder. The chamber was a mass of smoke and noise. Bas' senses tingled and flared. He focused on his breaths but none of their meditative practice would settle his mind.

It was only when hands appeared in front of him holding the Seeing Bowl did he realize the others had already began drinking from it. The red liquid inside sloshed against the impossibly dark rim. He didn't want to take it. Bas pushed down that thought and lifted the bowl from his sibling's hands. He brought it to his mouth and tipped the bowl.

The blood was cool as it ran down his throat. It tasted like water. Clear and tangy. The liquid sat in his stomach as Bas passed the Seeing Bowl to the next sibling. Relief eased some of the tension in his back.

Bas' eyes widened. The once cool blood was warming in his gut. It was getting hotter. Panic flared alongside it as the heat gave no indication of stopping the rising burning sensation. It burned from his gut all the way up his throat and to his mind and filled him with fire. Bas wanted to scream.

The chanting rang like shouting in his ears. The sounds took shape and words started to form in the clamour of noise.

The Seen, the Unseen.
All fall to the Seeing.
The Seen, the Unseen.
All fall to the Seeing.

The words repeated over and over as the blood spread through his limbs like flames. The red smoke thickened until the chamber disappeared into it. The noise, the pain all came to a crescendo and Bas didn't think he could last another second.

Then, it stopped.

Silence.

The burning subsided.

All Bas could see was red.

Then, the faint whistle of wind. It rolled over his skin and the red took shape as smoke once more before being blown away in the breeze.

Bas stood on a stone perch. The desert around him was clear and still. Bas spun looking around. Was this the vision? It felt so real.

He glanced up and the Sun Eye filled the sky. Bas stumbled and fell backwards, his eyes never straying from Ova's Sun Eye. It was huge, consuming the entire sky. And its burning gaze was fixed on Bas.

Then it blinked shut.

It did not pass through the sky and complete its watch as it did every day. It blinked its great eye *shut* and the desert plunged into darkness.

A purple light prickled to life on the horizon. Bas watched it and knew it was wrong. This was not the natural light of the World Turner but something else. The world lurched forward. The desert stretched and pulled as the city of Yontar came into view. It was impossible. The city was several days of travel away from the Settlement but there it was, standing before him. Dark purple light flooded it with a hazy glow.

All his meditative practices blanked from his mind in the frenzy of confusion and fear. There was no sign of life within the city. Somehow, he knew Yontar was dead and had been for some time.

Shutters sat askew with no firelight shining from within. Sand piled in the street corners as the desert fought to reclaim the bones of the dead city.

The Thousand Floor Palace stuck out as a spire from the city's top. A beacon and testament to Tarrisian strength. From the palace, a black shroud poured from the windows and doors like fog blooming outward, smothering the purple light and the city of Yontar both. Bas could only watch as everything was consumed by the darkness. It reached past the city and towards him. He did not run. He did not know what this shroud was but somehow he understood it, and there was no fleeing. This was darkness itself. There was no outrunning it.

The inky wave hit and plunged everything into a bluster-
ing black. The dark filled his lungs and he couldn't breathe.
He choked and coughed but he couldn't dislodge the
shroud.

Bas died in that darkness.

It was unlike anything he had felt before. All thought fell
away and feeling drained from his body like sand in a timer.
It reminded Bas of meditating. There was no pain, only
stillness.

And then nothing.

Liquid filled his lungs and Bas started as he felt his body
again. There was no time for confusion as he fought for life.
He clawed upwards and broke the surface of the pool dragging in air. Coughing and spluttering, Bas' mind whirled. He
was in a pool of blood. Bodies floated around him. He knew
them. All of them. The entire Settlement was dead.

Finally, Bas screamed.

He hadn't screamed since he was a child. It was raw and
painful on his already dry throat. The blood rippled around
him and the bodies bobbed in the red waves. He floundered
his way to the edge of the pool, where blood met sand.
Heaving, Bas crawled out of the pool and threw up. He
collapsed onto the sand breathing hard. The sky above was
purple and bright but neither of Ova's Eyes filled it. It was
just that unnatural purple light. That unsettled him more
than Ova's Eye appearing huge above him.

A hand grabbed his ankle. Bas didn't have time to look
down before he was pulled beneath the waves once more.

Bas sat up gasping.

"It's okay," Maut Desa said, laying a hand on his shoulder. "It's over. You're back."

Bas' heart hammered as he looked around wide eyed. He
was back in their sleeping chambers. Mauts wandered back
and forth as some of his siblings squirmed and screamed as
they slept. Little nooks where they slept were cut into the
cavern's walls, along with steps cut into the stone. Daylight
poured in from the slither of sky above them. Only a handful
of Bas' siblings had woken but they looked as startled as he
felt.

"Maut Desa I..." Bas started.

"No." She raised her hand. "Do not speak of what you
saw. The Seeing Bowl shows what it must to who it must."

Bas closed his mouth. But what did it mean? He remembered everything so vividly. It wasn't like remembering a dream as it was remembering yesterday. Ova's Sun Eye blinking shut. The dead city of Yontar. Darkness covering the land. The Urdahl people floating in a pool of their blood. Reining in his thoughts, Bas gulped and lay back. He couldn't show weakness. He had to settle his mind.

"Good," Maut Desa said. "Now, take this." She handed him a waterskin and walked off as another of his siblings woke, screaming.

Something bad was coming. Something that threatened them all. That much was clear but what was it? Why had he been shown as much and what could he do about it? Surely this was a vision to be shared with the elders. Those older and wiser who could help decipher it and stop this destruction and death.

But it was forbidden. The vision was for him and him alone.

Bas wondered if any of the others had a similar experience. Were they shown the devastation to come? The thought was reassuring. At least then he wouldn't be alone fighting this darkness. Bas took a draught from the waterskin and began to meditate, the screams of his siblings quieting.

Bas tried to let his mind go blank but flashes of the oncoming black wouldn't let him. He had meditated, walked, and gone through the breathing exercises. None of them helped alleviate this uneasy itch. He should be informing the elders. They should be planning for whatever was coming.

He needed their wisdom.

Elder Niru spent most of his time in contemplation or reading in the temple. If he was meditating he was not to be disturbed so Bas hoped he would find the elder in the temple archives.

Dust motes floated through the haze as Bas took to the steps, gazing up at the pillars outside the temple entrance. Ma-nivi, deity of knowledge and wisdom covered the walls and pillars. The owl-like deity was depicted in front of bowing scholars. Said to be one of the few deities that could speak their language, Ma-nivi passed to them the knowledge of parchment making and scroll work in ancient times. Now, its likeness could be found across Tarris and beyond on libraries and places of learning. Just seeing the deity settled some of Bas' worry. If he was to find wisdom, he would find it here.

The entry chamber was a high-ceilinged space with a massive floating orb of light. Bands of metal spun around it. The orb never extinguished or dimmed. The Urdahl had never learned the secret of its light. An ancient mystery but one they were grateful for. Many Urdahl read in silence on benches and at tables that were strewn amongst more pillars. Only the low thrum of the light orb could be heard within the walls of the temple.

Bas made his way into the main chamber. Decrepit shelves filled the floor. Their splintering wood holding all the knowledge and teachings of the Urdahl people. A dais stood like a tower at the far side of the temple holding aloft a life-sized statue of Ma-nivi. It wasn't uncommon for elders to pray at the base of the statue when looking for guidance.

Walking up the shelving, Bas peered into each row in turn looking for the elder. The original temple had been empty but the first of the Urdahl turned it into a library and place of learning. Bas always thought the seating and rows of shelves blocked out some of the majesty of the temple. Etched into the floor and walls were ancient tapestries that depicted some of the first words of Ma-nivi and the beginnings of the old tongue marked the spaces between the murals. Some believed that it was Ma-nivi who created the old tongue so humans could talk to one another and the deity.

Elder Niru stood in one of the far rows where the older texts were kept. He held a book close to his face, eyes squinting in the low light. On the cover, the illustration of a hollowed-out apple glinted in the firelight. Atop the ruins in the feast cavern and lit by the Great Fire, Elder Niru looked to be an ancient among men but here within the stacks of the library he was but a man. Bas moved up the aisle quietly and bowed. He only raised when Elder Niru closed his book and motioned him to do so.

"Ah, Bas," Elder Niru said. "I didn't imagine I would see you or any of your siblings today. Most go into meditation after drinking from the Seeing Bowl."

"That is why I sought you out, Elder. I need your advice on what I saw in the blood," Bas said.

"You know it is forbidden to discuss what is seen."

"I know elder but I really think—"

Elder Niru raised a hand. "I cannot. If I was to know what you have seen, I would have been shown it when I drank from the bowl."

"I understand that elder but could it be that I was shown it to share with you? I've seen things that I believe are yet to come and it affects a lot more than myself," Bas said.

Niru sighed then flicked his head towards the seating laid out in rows at the edges of the chamber. "Come."

The elder groaned as he lowered himself onto a stone bench. His face flickered to one of strain and eased. But the expression thrust Bas back into the vision where Elder Niru had been one of those floating dead in the blood pool. In the vision he couldn't put a name to the face but now it was so clear. He felt the blood drain from his face.

"Bas," Niru said, "the Seeing Bowl isn't something we discuss and one of the reasons why we don't is because we don't truly understand it."

Had Bas misheard? A fundamental part of the Urdahl was the testing and half of that was drinking from the Seeing Bowl. Everything was to become clear after seeing the vision but Bas felt more clouded than ever. And if the elders didn't even understand its power...

"We believe it is a vision bestowed to us by the blood of a deity but which deity we do not know. What is seen in the blood is never discussed but some of the elders claim to have seen the past. Something that they have confirmed with the records in these very walls." The elder gestured to the library.

"Most say they saw purpose and meaning. Given flashes of what they were meant to accomplish in this world," Niru said. He stroked his beard and stared at Bas. "None of the living elders have seen into the future but it was said that an elder many generations ago foresaw events yet to come."

"It—"

"Stop," Elder Niru said sharply. "If you truly saw days to come and you're not content with them then you must seek out a way to prevent these events. And you must do it alone. The vision is yours and yours alone."

"What if I don't know what to do?" Bas said.

"*A wrong step can be redirected. Remaining still is for the mind not the feet,"* Elder Niru recited.

Bas nodded. It wasn't the response he had hoped for but it was what he had expected. Urdahl pride themselves on individual strength. One was to take hardship in stride and deal with it themselves.

"Thank you for your time, Elder Niru," Bas said.

The elder bowed politely and Bas stood and matched the gesture.

It was the familiar grunts and cracking of staffs that drew Bas from wandering the wind tunnels and into the training grounds. Urdahl sparred between the beams of sunlight in the cavern. The smell of sweat swelled in a sickly stench. Some Urdahl were hanging from the rock by ropes and had others punch their torso like Bas had the day before.

Each struggled. Each pushed themselves beyond their limits. Who was he to ask for help when his brothers and sisters fought?

Making his way through the cavern and out the back he came into a smaller space where burning coals stretched out across the middle of the room. The 712th year siblings were back again today training on the fire walk.

Steam plumed from the narrow straight of coals that the children had to walk across without screaming. Only once one could pass without making a sound could they advance to the next stage. Bas still remembered the surge of elation at crossing the flames as silent as the stone around them.

One of the children was halfway across with sweat running down their scalp. Their face was red and looked like it would burst under the strain of trying to keep silent. The coals hissed as the child set one foot in front of the other.

Most of the 712th siblings sat on the ground, feet held aloft. Bas could see their blisters and burns from across the chamber. There were whimpering and quiet cries. The child crossed and dropped to the ground clutching at their feet.

"Good. Eri, you next," Elder Cino said.

The fear on Eri's face was palpable as he stepped up to the edge of the fire walk. He looked at the coals like they were the burning eyes of demons peering from Duat itself. Glancing up, Eri caught sight of Bas. Bas nodded and the boy's face steeled.

Eri walked onto the burning coals.

His eyes bulged but he made no sound as he took the first couple of steps across the fire walk. Bas thought of the story and of the hero. Was that what Eri was thinking about now? Was he imagining himself as the hero from the story?

There is strength in lies, Bas thought.

Could he be the one to save the Settlement? Yes, he told himself. He was of the Urdahl. Bas had to be strong and bear the weight so those who followed could flourish. That was of the Urdahl.

He watched as Eri threw everything into moving forward. The boy didn't look at the stretch of fire in front of him but at his feet and he took another step.

Bas' next step was completing his testing. For now, that was what he needed to focus on. Tomorrow he would cross the Passage of the High Pass and prove his worth as an Urdahl. One step at a time.

Eri completed the fire walk. As he stepped off, the boy collapsed and screamed.

3

Passage of the High Pass

"Crossing the desert of existence is one of cresting and falling."
- Urdahl Proverb

The day began with the searing call of a horn. Most of the 700th year siblings were eating their morning meal when it sounded. Bas stood in line to the Great Fire. He turned to Mei who nodded. Bas cursed himself for not getting up earlier to eat breakfast as he left the line and made his way back to their sleeping chamber to grab his supplies.

The siblings gathered atop a rocky plateau out in the open desert. The reddening morning sky was yet to become un-bearably hot but Bas knew he would be out in the Sun Eye's gaze for most of the day and relished the cool. He wore his best travel gear. Light brown jerkin that would defend against blade and claw but it was not too heavy to be en-cumbering. A light pack was strapped to his back filled with supplies. There was little guidance on what to bring during the Passage of the High Pass but it wasn't as secretive as the Seeing Bowl, so most of his siblings had been talking with the older Urdahl collecting advice.

Mei stood at his side wearing similar light traveling gear and a pack on her back. Her face ever-stoic and eyes fixed on the horizon. She had changed since the Seeing Bowl. Her joviality had sharpened to something else. Whatever she saw in the blood had focused her mind.

Bas had woken during the night to find her reading by firelight in the late hours. He had gone to her then, creeping across the sleeping chamber to her bedside. She held a meaty tome called *The Dark between the Light*.

"Are you ready?" Bas whispered as his siblings slept around them. It was a foolish question. Urdahl only spoke when the words were worth uttering and these were not. But he wanted to see that resolve in her eyes. He wanted to feel that same resolve.

She turned. The raising of her eyebrow told Bas she thought his words foolish, too.

"Of course. Are you not?"

"I am," Bas said. "I just wondered." He gestured to the book.

"I'm going over edible plants in the area so I can pack less food," she said.

Bas nodded. It was a good idea. One of the few pieces of advice they had been given from the older years was to pack light.

Mei glanced at those around her and then back to Bas. "Bas." There was something strained in her voice. Few would pick up on it but Bas did. "Remember the ways of the Urdahl."

"What do you mean?"

"The Passage of the High Pass is a test of strength. Strength of mind and muscle," Mei said.

"I know."

There was something in the way she held herself. Something only an Urdahl could see. A slight tightness in her shoulders. The angle of her head tilted away from him. A tension unseen to most.

"Good," she said after a moment. "Now, go to sleep. Let me read."

He went back to bed.

None of that strain from the night before had carried to today. Mei was stone. Bas wondered at what might have been bothering her. Nerves? It seemed unlikely.

Three elders stood in front of the siblings, Elder Niru a step ahead of the two others. Niru cleared his throat and all conversation came to a halt. He took a moment to look over the 700th year siblings before nodding.

"You have sipped from the Seeing Bowl. No longer should you strive to be seen or unseen, as you are now the seeing. Sometimes purpose and meaning become clear in an instant. Powers beyond the comprehending showing you why you are here. Other times it is cryptic and hidden. With only vague implications.

"As Urdahl we do not rush. Time will meet us. The future will come soon enough and with it will come wisdom," Elder Niru said. His gaze swept across them, hovering over Bas for a moment. "We continue. We walk on through the sands of time. Today those sands have brought you to the Passage of the High Pass.

"You have no doubt heard about some of the details from past year siblings but I will go over the event. You have until sunrise tomorrow to make your way over the high pass ridge and to the nesting place of the artengo. There, you will steal an egg and bring it to the Great Fire."

The 700th year siblings looked across the desert to the rocky plateau. It was a mountainous formation that reached far across the dunes. But it was far from flat. They would need to scale the high pass and make their way through the uneven ridge fighting the fauna that hid in the shade of the mountain and its crevices.

The artengo nests were on the far side. The giant blue-feathered birds blended into the sky above so their prey didn't even know they were being hunted until it was too late. And they were fiercely defensive of their young. Not to mention that the behemoth birds were large enough to eat a person whole.

There was an opening back into the Settlement on the far side of the high pass ridge that led directly into the feast cavern where the Great Fire always roared. Fighting an artengo was madness but if they stole the egg and snuck down the side of the ridge, they could escape into the Settlement.

"And the first three Urdahl to return will be rewarded with the first pick of their roles," Elder Niru said.

This drew some eyes back from the high pass. After they passed the testing the 700th year would become full Urdahls which meant they needed to take up roles in the Settlement. Getting the first pick of one's role in life was an enticing prize. All jobs within the Settlement had to be filled and often Urdahl were put into roles unsuited to their interests.

"There are only two rules: do not fatally harm another Urdahl and return before first light tomorrow," Elder Niru said. "Those who do not return before then will be dropped into a younger year as one of the disgraced Unaged."

There were only a few Unaged among the Urdahl but they were selected for the most unsavoury roles within the Settlement and few were seen talking with the Unaged. Once an Urdahl was Unaged, there was no return. No second chance.

Bas wanted to clench his fists. He wanted to adjust his pack. He wanted to shift his weight between his feet. He did none of that. Instead, he stood and he breathed slowly steadying his mind. This was it. All he had trained for.

"You may begin."

The Urdahl burst into motion. Bas ran for the edge of the rock formation and dove off. He pulled out his glider as he fell. The air caught the fabric and it puffed out with an audible *thwack*. Mei floated down at his side with her own glider. Other Urdahl had the same thought and glided slowly to the sands below but a good amount of Urdahl were clambering down the side of the stone.

Good, Bas thought watching them move down the rock. It was unlikely they would recover from the oversight. The gliders were already carrying some of the Urdahl towards the high pass and those who had to climb down wouldn't be able to catch them.

About thirty of his siblings had thought of the glider too. Including Rfan and her partner, Cerl. It was no secret that Rfan and Bas were the strongest amongst the 700th siblings. She would be his main competition if he wanted the first pick of the roles.

Bas hit the sand running. Others spread out. Some ran towards the edges of the high pass, no doubt thinking it faster to stay on the desert level and climb up to the nesting spot at the other end of the plateau. What they didn't know was that the rocks were sheer and difficult to climb. It was a much better choice to climb up this side and make their way through the mountainous plateau.

Reaching the high pass, Bas leapt and started climbing. Mei grunted as she clambered up after him. The jagged rocks made for easy climbing but one glance upward revealed the size of the task ahead.

Despite the rock face being in the shade, sweat beaded on Bas' brow. The dry dusty rock was becoming slippery beneath his sweat slicked fingers. Adrenaline and the buzz of the testing had him pushing too hard. He would have to rein himself in if he was to hold a consistent pace across the pass.

His preparations ran through his mind. Bas quietened it. His muscles strained as he reached up to the next ledge. He listened to the rasp of his breaths, even but too fast. Dragging himself atop the next ledge, Bas stopped to catch his breath. Mei was only a second after him. She also looked drained.

"We're ahead of the others," Bas said. He took a waterskin from his pack and took a deep draught.

"For now," Mei said between her heavy breathing. She scanned the cliff face. "We're a quarter of the way up. Some have already made it past us."

"We'll catch them on the ridge," Bas said. "They're wearing themselves out too quickly."

Mei nodded.

They sat for a couple minutes longer before continuing their arduous climb. Mei moved out from beneath Bas as dust puffed out at his steps. They stopped another time, noting their siblings' progress. Some had only just made it to the base of the rock.

Eventually, Bas pulled himself up into the Sun Eye's gaze and onto the high pass. He lay flat feeling the warmth soothe some of his aches and pains. This was not the top of the pass. That was a thin ridge but Mei and Bas had decided against moving across that. It left them too open to attack. The artengo would surely see them and they would have nowhere to run. But here, rocky passes and ledges moved towards the nesting area in relative shelter.

Bas sat up, waiting for Mei. She had fallen behind. In the meantime, Bas thought to get the lay of the land.

He leapt onto a rock and shimmied up the side to get a better view. Here the pass was laid out before him, stretching out towards where artengo nested. It was too far to see the nests or any of the birds.

He looked to the sky but the blue was still and undisturbed. Trailing his gaze across it, he landed on Yontar. The city sat on the horizon in the haze of the Sun Eye.

This place. It felt oddly similar. He hadn't ever climbed

the high pass before. Perhaps another perch had a similar rock formation? Then it struck him. This was where he stood in his vision.

Bas suddenly felt cold. He shielded his eyes from the Sun Eye, squinting at the far-off city.

A black shroud emanated from Yontar.

Bas froze. He blinked trying to shake the illusion but the black smoke didn't shift.

"Hey. Do you see anything?" Mei called.

"Look at Yontar!"

Mei glanced over but there was no recognition on her face. "What about it?"

"Don't you see it?"

"See what?" Mei asked.

Was this in his head? They had learned that built up stress can cause hallucinations. Perhaps the testing was affecting him more than he thought. Or was this a remnant of the vision from the Seeing Bowl? What did it mean?

He thought about the red pool of blood filled with the Urdahl. Was that too going to come to pass?

It's in my head, Bas thought. *It must be.*

He turned away from the city. Bas tried to steel himself but Mei could see that he was shaken.

"What is it?" Mei asked.

"I thought I saw something, that's all," Bas said.

Mei stared at him. She could see through his lie but she didn't push on the point. "Let's get moving, then."

They took off at a jog. The stone crunched under their feet as they ran along the narrow walkway. Mei slid to a stop in front of him and Bas almost barrelled into her. A rockfall had destroyed part of the path. Rocks skittered down the gap, kicked up by their movement.

Mei glanced down. Her face paled. As children they were trained at heights to shake the natural fear but it was one that Mei hadn't mastered. She had never admitted it but Bas noted his friend's discomfort anytime they practiced atop a plateau.

"I'll go first," Bas said. He laid a hand on Mei's shoulder and she stiffened.

"Why? I'm fine." Mei shook him off.

Mei didn't hesitate before taking a few steps back and then sprinting towards the gap. She launched herself over the drop and onto the far side. She landed hard skittering across the rock. From the far side, Bas could see her breathing heavily. It was of the Urdahl to not show weakness and Mei was stubborn at the best of times.

Bas blew out a breath and took a running start. He kicked off the edge. Weightless. The stone sent a jolt through Bas as he tumbled to the other side of the path. Then they were off again.

They didn't run into any other Urdahl. Bas guessed they had found other paths through the ridge or into the caverns that tunnelled through its length. He had thought of using the caverns and tunnels as they were more direct but they were said to be maze-like and Bas didn't trust that they wouldn't get lost. Creatures were also said to roam the caves and caverns of the high pass. Few clung to the outside in the glaring Sun Eye's gaze. But inside, where it was damp and cool? One would find more than lizards and scardrae hidden in the dark.

Again their path eroded to little more than a slither. Bas stepped out onto the ridge first. He shimmied onward, hugging the rock without so much as a glance to the fall. Bas leapt the last of the distance and turned to Mei. She swallowed, gazing at the dizzying distance.

Mei reached a tentative foot onto the ledge before yanking her body back.

"It's okay," Bas said. He met her eyes. "Just look at me."

Urdahl didn't talk about their weaknesses. They were to hide their fears so they couldn't be used against them. Mei screwed her face up and then forced it back to neutral, suppressing the embarrassment from her face.

"Go on," Mei said. "I will catch up."

She was slowing their progress and she knew it.

"I will wait. I need a break from running anyway."

Mei looked like she was going to scold him but kept her mouth shut.

Keeping her eyes on Bas, Mei crept onto the ledge. He should have gone on. He should have left her there with her weakness but he couldn't. Bas knew she would fall behind if he left her.

Her foot scraped along the stone.

"Good," Bas said.

Mei's exhale trembled as she kept her gaze fixed on Bas.

Searching fingers ran across the stone. Her foot hit a rock and it pinged out over the chasm below. Mei followed the rock and glanced down before Bas could tell her not to. Her eyes bulged and breath caught. She was losing her balance.

The world knocked from its axis. Bas always thought he would relax in times of stress but fear had him in a choke hold as he reached out over the edge. He grabbed Mei's jerkin and yanked her forward. Bas and Mei fell in a tumble of limbs. A strangled gasp broke from Bas as life surged back into his body.

They lay there for some time breathing hard. Swallowing the nausea, Bas turned to Mei. She was rubbing her face and taking long slow breaths.

"You should have kept going," she said.

"I needed a break."

She stared at him, keeping her expression neutral. Bas couldn't tell if she was thankful or indignant that he had stayed. "Come on. We need to move."

Bas watched Mei's back as she leapt from rock to rock clambering up an incline. Bas followed. They continued running in silence. The shade of the rock wall to their right, keeping them cool.

"Why didn't you keep going?" Mei asked, falling into stride at Bas' side.

"You're my friend," Bas said. "I want you at my side when we finish."

Mei thought over that for a second. "It is not Urdahl to help another in training. It trains us to rely on others and slows our progress to overcome adversity."

"Being Urdahl means being strong. It's about standing after being knocked down. I wanted to make sure you got back up."

Mei opened her mouth then closed it again. "Thank you," she said.

Bas nodded.

Cresting a ridge, they came onto a long, flat opening on the plateau. Rock walls acted as wind breaks and a crevice snaked through the rock as a jagged crack. Bas peered into the dark. It fell away to an unseeable bottom. Bas leapt over it and Mei followed closely behind. It wasn't the same as seeing the drop to the sand below.

Bas was about to start running again when Rfan and her

friend, Cerl, stepped out from behind a rock formation. Bas halted. There was malice in their eyes. Rfan clearly didn't want to risk the race and planned to disable Bas and Mei here. There was a no fatal harm rule but there was no rule against fighting and incapacitating others.

Rfan strolled towards them.

"Afraid you will lose the race?" Bas asked.

"This is of the Urdahl," Rfan said. Neither she nor Cerl had reached for their weapons but Bas watched them for any sign of motion towards the swords at their belts. "Anticipating and strategy are of the Urdahl."

Bas' fingers twitched, ready to grab the staff attached to his back.

Fingers tugged at his jerkin. Looking around, Bas saw the guilt on Mei's face as she yanked him back.

His feet slid on the rock.

Panic rode up his throat.

Bas lost his footing and fell into the crevice as Mei looked away.

Battering against the stone wall, Bas fell into the darkness.

4

Stillness of the Fallen

"Only when one can still themselves in a storm can they see through it."
- Urdahl Proverb

It was of the Urdahl. Bas should have anticipated this. The top contenders were Rfan, Cerl, and Bas. By making a deal with Rfan, Mei all but guaranteed her spot as one of the top three. Mei made the smart choice.

Bas didn't feel despair as he lay in the dark. He didn't feel betrayed. Rather, it was acceptance that filled him. He was outmanoeuvred and that was his weakness, his fault.

The hiss of sand echoed around him. It was too dark to see his surroundings but the calming noise told Bas he wasn't unconscious. The crack of burning white sky too far to push back the pooling black. He hadn't moved yet but the fog in his mind and liquid tickling the back of his head whispered that he was done. He wasn't going to make it to the Great Fire by first light.

Something in Bas eased at the thought. There was no need to fight and push himself if he had already lost. Bas let out a breath. Shouldn't he be feeling defeated? Frustrated? He had trained his entire life for the testing and now he had failed. He would no doubt become one of the Unaged and shunned for the rest of his life.

Why then did he feel at peace?

His mind fell to Eri and his book. Eri always seemed to be at peace. No matter the day nor the activity, Bas was sure the boy would be smiling. *Peace of mind and soul.* The Urdahl tenet that wasn't one of the written proverbs but often it was written onto the title page of their books and scrolls. It was the ultimate practice and most sought after. And yet, often the most overlooked. In that way, Eri was more Urdahl than some of the elders. They practiced peace of mind throughout their lives but it came naturally to Eri.

He was impulsive, foolish, and revealed his emotions too often, but sometimes Bas wondered if the boy had figured out something the elders hadn't. He felt it now in the stillness of his fall. There was more to being Urdahl than the testing. To be Urdahl was to find life and joy separate from that which happened around you.

Bas stared into the black. Eri wouldn't have lain there. He would have already gotten up and been searching for a way out. Was the testing all he had? Was it the only reason he had to rise again?

Stillness in the storm. Determination from defeat. Strength from ashes.

Bas pushed himself up. Not to complete the testing but because he was Urdahl. Because he had been shown a vision in blood. Because he loved those in the Settlement; Eri, the elders, the mauts, and his siblings, even Mei and Rfan. And Bas wasn't going to lie there in the dark and let the vision come to pass.

He waited for the wave of nausea to pass before attempting to pull himself to his feet. The stone wall was cool and sharp. Bas pressed against it and started to walk. There was no climbing out of this darkness so he would have to go through it.

After a few steps his foot hit something hard. *My staff,* Bas thought and reached down to pick it up. As his fingers searched through the dark he realized it had snapped in two. He picked up the two halves, the two pieces of wood clacking against one another. Bas slid them into his belt and continued on.

The sound of a sandfall grew louder as Bas sidestepped through the cave. A sandfall could mean another way out. He just needed to make sure he didn't walk into it and get dragged into the stream and suffocate. One hand reaching into the dark, he searched ever onward.

Light leaked around the edge of the cave wall. But it wasn't the light of the Sun Eye. It was a cool light. The cavern wall curved and Bas followed it around the corner.

Adrias, blue luminescent mushrooms, covered the cave walls. The mushrooms glowed and lit the cavern in a soft turquoise light. As if the light brought Bas back to the world around him, cuts flared across his skin and pain flooded through his muscles and down the back of his head. A wave of nausea sent the cave spinning.

Bas eased himself down onto the rock waiting for his vision to settle. The cave didn't lead upward like Bas had hoped. It led deeper into the stone ridge. Adrias lighting the way with their pulsing blue glow. The caverns within the high ridge pass were renowned for being difficult to traverse. The rocks fell sharply downward. If he hadn't taken the fall, Bas might have been able to slide down the face of the rock but given that he didn't know the extent of his injuries, he would have to lower himself down slowly.

Glancing around the stark stone cavern, it was clear he would have to use what he brought for any cave diving. He unslung his pack and opened it. Bas blew out a breath. His waterskin had punctured and leaked his water all over his supplies.

He ate the soggy bread before more of it broke off in a slop. His glider was wet but remained undamaged. That was good but the cavern was too narrow to use it to get down. He stuck the strips of dried meat into his belt and pulled out the last item: a tan cloak. He had brought it to blend in with the rock and hide from the artengo. Bas whipped the cloak with a *thwack* and water droplets spattered the rock.

He threw away his empty pack and stepped up to the edge. Using the end of the cloak, he tied it to a rock and tossed it off the sheer rock. It didn't reach the bottom but it was far enough that he could drop the rest of the way. Clutching the fabric, he stepped backwards out onto the cave wall and started to descend. After coming to the end of the cloak, Bas pressed his feet against the stone and slid the rest of the way down. His legs didn't give as he landed hard in a puff of dust and dirt.

The cloak clung to the rock just out of reach. Bas turned to face the blue cave.

The cavern stripped him of supplies as Mei had stripped him of the testing. But Bas knew it was what was inside that drove him, and that could not be stripped away.

A howl and scuffle of movement came from further in the cavern. Bas dropped low and listened. Everything went silent. It was more than the terrain that dissuaded the Urdahl from using the caves. Bas pulled out the two pieces of his staff which clattered to the ground. He bent down and picked up the pieces as well as a rock. The staff had broken almost perfectly in half.

Breaking is an act of creation as much as it is destruction.

It was one of Rfan's favourite proverbs to recite when training with the younger year siblings.

Bas used the rock to peel away the wood at the end of the staff until it came to a point. He did the same with the second piece wearing away the wood until it was sharp enough to pierce flesh. With that done, Bas twirled the two halves. They didn't have the fluidity of the staff but they would kill just the same.

Bas picked a handful of the glowing adrias mushrooms to ward off the dark and waded on. The adrias would glow for an hour after being picked.

That would have to do.

The weak blue light did a poor job illuminating the cave as less adrias grew on the walls. Bas' footsteps rang farther away, giving Bas the sense that the cavern was widening. However once he came to another edge, he realized the cave opened up into a large cavern below him. Adrias grew in patches across the cavern below, only lighting some of the space. Some of the corners lay in darkness. Against the far wall, the sandfall hissed.

And beside it was a crack of white light. A way out.

A shaky breath escaped Bas' lips. He hadn't realised how concerned he was about not finding a way out.

Bas dropped into the cave and ran for the opening. He must have clambered halfway down the high pass as he made his way through this cavern but he could climb his way back up and—

Instinct took over as movement on the edges of Bas' vision surged towards him. He rolled backwards just as the irkan snapped where he had been not a moment before. The six-legged creature's head cracked as it swivelled to face him. Irkan didn't have a call. They made little noise as they hunted through the caves of the desert and their movement sounded like groaning rock to mask their whereabouts. The irkan was three times Bas' height with its long legs reaching five or six spans wide. Even in the dim light, Bas could make out the rock like skin of the beast. Twenty beady black eyes lined its snouted face, all fixed on Bas. Known as the great stone spiders, irkan were rare and Bas had only ever seen sketches. But they were unmistakable.

The irkan sprang towards Bas who dove forward. He dug his two makeshift daggers upward as the irkan passed overhead. They barely marked the hard scale-like skin, dragging little more than markings across its belly. The irkan landed and whipped one of its legs out. It battered into Bas, sending him flying. He smacked into the cave wall, knocking the air from his lungs. His eyes bulged as he landed in a heap.

Bas' sense flared. The irkan was already in the air when he glanced up. He rolled out the way but felt the irkan clip his back. Bas stifled a scream as he felt claws tear through his flesh. Rocks dug into the open wound as he bounced across the ground.

He pushed himself onto his hands and knees. The irkan watched him. It stood side on to Bas but he saw movement in those black eyes. Like something was swimming beneath the surface. The irkan didn't attack but bowed its head, the front half of its body lowering with the sound of groaning stone.

The Urdahl had thought these were mindless creatures but there was intelligence in those eyes. It respected Bas. He was silent and didn't scream and flee like the irkan's usual prey.

Bas stood on shaky legs taking the respite. Blood ran from a gash along his forehead. The beast was too quick. He didn't have the chance to fight back when all he could do was avoid its attacks. He needed to find a way to distract it or slow it down. But even if he did, his broken staff wasn't enough to pierce the creature's thick hide.

The irkan charged. Making a split decision, Bas turned and clambered up the rock. The cavern shook as the irkan battered into the cave wall. Bas leapt higher up the rock and started chipping into a stalactite. The irkan buried its legs in the rock wall. Cracks snaked through the cavern as the creature scuttled up towards him. The stone spear finally came free and Bas leapt.

He was weightless.

The stalactite dropped as he fell and sliced into the irkan's side. The once silent beast squealed as it fell back, six legs flailing. Bas landed hard, his legs buckling beneath him. He remained silent. If he were to make a noise the irkan would surely attack.

Staggering to the side of the cavern, Bas watched the irkan rip the stalactite free.

Bas took to the rock wall once more climbing high into a darker part of the cave where the adrias' blue light faded to shadow.

The beast stomped on the stalactite, grinding it to dust. The sound echoed through the cavern. Bas froze. The irkan plodded into the centre of the cave, scanning the rock. It moved with the surety of a beast that hadn't been threatened its entire life. It didn't matter that the irkan couldn't see Bas. He would have to come out eventually and Bas was a mere human.

A broken human with a shattered weapon.

That was no threat to the irkan.

The irkan circled the cave. It slammed its legs into the wall sending a shudder through the rock. It grew ever closer. Every couple steps it smashed its leg into the wall, a tremor pulsing outward through the cave. Once it got close enough the irkan would knock Bas from his hiding spot.

Crack.

It took two steps closer.

Crack.

Bas leant into the fear.

Crack.

He felt it rise and fall.

Crack.

Closer.

CRACK.

Sharpen and dull.

CRACK.

Closer.

CRACK.

The irkan was right below him.

Now.

Bas released his grip and fell towards the beast. The irkan glanced up in time to see the bleeding, broken Urdahl before the two halves of his staff burst through the creature's eyes. They popped and spat black ooze at Bas. He felt the irkan's skull crack and the hafts reach its soft insides.

The beast collapsed and thudded against the floor.

Bas' rasping breath bounced around the quiet cave. He yanked out his two weapons and flicked them, blood spattering the walls. Breathing hard, Bas tucked them back into his belt and headed for the crack of light.

Sunlight warmed his skin as he peered across the desert to the Sun Eye as it dipped towards the horizon. Bruises ached. Cuts stung. Blood dried on his skin. Bas was parched and tired and hungry.

"Breaking is an act of creation as much as it is destruction," Bas whispered and he started to climb.

Eri watched as more 700th year siblings returned. The rhythmic chanting echoed around the Wayup cavern that led out to the desert. Firelight flickered along the walls of the cavern as the Sun Eye sank towards the horizon. Urdahl lined up along either side, bowing their heads as the Urdahl returned from their testing. Most carried artengo eggs, strength sharp on their features. But a few returned with a weariness they could not hide and no egg to show their prowess. There were always a handful that failed every turning season. They would join the Unaged that would be shunned among the Urdahl.

"Stop," Maut Tera said.

Eri stilled his jittering leg. That wasn't of the Urdahl but he couldn't mask his concern. Bas should have been among the first to return and now half of his siblings had returned before him.

He's hurt. He's out there by himself and he's hurt.

Eri couldn't stop his worries. He thought Bas was working with Mei but she returned with Rfan as one of the first three.

Eri had asked her where Bas was and Mei just shrugged.

Eri remembered the time his siblings had been tasked with climbing through a set of caves as part of their training. Eri had fallen and twisted his ankle but his siblings had left him. It was not Urdahl to help one who was meant to be training and getting stronger. If they helped him, he wouldn't learn. Eri had lain there for a couple hours before mustering the strength to start crawling.

Then he came. Bas had appeared and supported him all the way back, even though he would be ridiculed by his siblings and told off by the elders for doing so.

Another Urdahl walked into the cave. A bloody gash ran down his shoulder but she held aloft an egg and the chanting surged. Eri looked past her to the darkening sky.

Where are you, Bas?

He didn't have long now. As light faded, so did it fade from Bas' chances of becoming a fully-fledged Urdahl.

Come on.

5

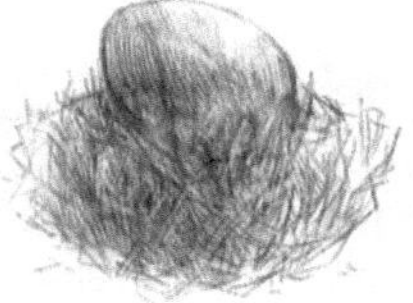

The Egg

"From ashes comes armour."
- Urdahl Proverb

The light fled from Bas, running up the rock face as the Sun Eye sank behind the horizon. The high pass was steeper here and he struggled to find purchase in the rock. As gaps in the stone grew smaller, Bas used the two halves of his staff as spikes that he stabbed into the crevices to pull himself up. There were no ledges to take breaks on.

Darkness had descended by the time Bas reached the top. His arms trembled as he pulled himself onto the ledge. A lizard scampered off as he brushed the dust from his jerkin. The other Urdahl would be at the nests by now. No doubt finding ways to sneak in and steal an egg before the artengo noticed them. And Bas still had the high pass ridge to cross. He wondered if Mei and Rfan were already back at the Great Fire celebrating their win.

From this part of the ridge, Yontar was clear on the horizon. An ember in the black of dark hour when both the Sun Eye and Moon Eye were not in the sky. But even in firelight, the shroud of darkness clung to the city like a blotch in Bas' eye. He wondered if he would always see the city that way now. Was this a constant reminder from the Seeing Bowl about his vision?

Bas had to go to Yontar. He had to find what was causing the darkness. But if he failed the testing, he would become one of the Unaged and they were banned from leaving the Settlement.

Dark hour would end soon and the Moon Eye would light the world anew. Was that enough time to make it to the nests?

Dwelling is an idle mind, Bas thought as he pushed on.

Artengo nests were unlike any other nests. The birds scraped into the rock creating craters. Then they killed kiren and other creatures of the desert bringing their carcasses back to the nests to use as bedding for their eggs. It was no wonder artengo were such a violent species when they were born in blood and flesh.

Bas peered from behind his cover at the nesting site. Artengo did not eat one another's eggs so they nested together as it was easier to protect against the few creatures that would dare to try and steal from them. Their silver talons gleamed in the moonlight. The rest of Bas' siblings must have already passed through as several of the craters were empty aside from the rotting carcasses.

The Moon Eye was dipping towards the horizon. Soon it would be the dark hour and if he hoped to return to the feast cavern before first light, he would need to glide off the high pass ridge before then.

Artengo roamed around their eggs. Some sat upon their nest of gore. The deep blue birds didn't hunt at night so it was unlikely any were flying above. Still, paranoia brought Bas' gaze to the skies, but there was only darkness and a speckling of stars.

Bas took a deep breath and started climbing. He clung to the side of a natural tower of stone that was covered in char-ah flowers. The small red flowers had deep roots that snaked through the rock and weakened its structural integrity. Bas slid out his broken staff and started hacking at the cracks in the rock. Just as the stone was about to collapse, Bas clambered back down and ran far from the crumbling tower.

The groan of rock scraping against rock crescendoed into a bone shaking *crack*. The top of the tower came crashing down sending up a plume of dust. The artengo squealed. Several flew over to where the rock lay in pieces.

Bas crept along the edge of the high pass ridge, running on his haunches. The birds squawked at each other. Bas approached a crater. Inside, a gleaming alabaster egg sat amongst the skeletal remains of several kiren. The putrid stench of decay hit Bas like a staff to the face. He stepped back, momentarily disoriented. Blowing out a breath, Bas steeled himself and slid down the side of the crater.

His boots and hands were covered in gore as he pressed through to the egg. Bas avoided looking down as each footstep squelched.

The egg was the size of his head and cool to the touch. If the artengo returned now Bas would join the dead at his feet. He knew he should hurry. He knew he should rush out of the crater but Bas couldn't help but take a moment and strain his hearing to listen for the artengo. Their squawking sounded far off.

Holding the egg under one arm, Bas clambered back out of the nest.

In the distance, he saw the artengo squabbling around his distraction. He had worried it wouldn't hold their attention for long but the artengo pecked through the remains for the small creatures who lived within the cracks of the stone. Bas ran behind a rock and ducked out of sight.

He had done it.

He had *done it*.

Bas' heart hammered. He held out the egg. It wasn't smooth like he had expected. Instead there was a coarseness to the shell.

I am of the Urdahl.

He had always thought of himself as Urdahl but to be proven *right*. To *know* that he was of the Urdahl. Elation flushed through him like a cool breeze. Strength steeled his limbs. Now he needed to get back to the Settlement before first light.

Bas carefully placed the egg down and unwrapped his glider from his belt. Stealing the egg was the easy part. Now he had to get across the nesting area and leap off the far side of the plateau.

But there was no way of doing that without being seen. Bas strapped the egg against his chest and slid out the two hafts of his staff.

Then he started to run.

He tore through the nesting area. The patter of his footsteps were mostly masked by the fighting birds. A caw broke through the snapping of birds. He'd been spotted. Bas turned just in time to see razor sharp talons headed right for his face. Diving to the right, Bas flicked his sharpened staff end. It scraped along the beast's side making it squeal in pain.

Artengo heads spun and seven sets of amber eyes fell on him, then shifted to the egg strapped to his chest.

Chaos erupted.

Some shot straight for him. Others took to the air. Several more artengo appeared from their craters. Bas dove out of the way of the first. He felt the wing of the artengo brush past him, the velocity sending him sprawling. Bas rolled onto his back bringing up his half staffs just in time to catch the talons of another artengo.

The bird flicked its talons and cawed in frustration as Bas kept jerking from side to side. If he hadn't attached the egg to his chest the artengo would have skewered him but Bas could see the worry in the bird's stance. Its wings were rigid. Veins bulged on the beast's neck. It didn't want to damage the egg.

Bas swiped his makeshift weapon and it ripped into the artengo's claws. It howled and flew upward. Wasting no time, Bas rose and continued his headlong sprint for the end of the plateau.

An artengo rushed at him from above. Bas leapt but felt the cold sting of the razor-sharp talons catching his calf. Suppressing a scream, Bas tumbled, careful to land on his side and not the egg. He dragged air into his lungs. The cool cut rising to a burning. It was deep. He felt the muscle pulsate and scream. Bas flopped onto his back. This would be it. The artengo wouldn't risk letting him get away again. He was dead.

One of the great blue birds dove for him.

"Bas!" a voice called.

Bas' head spun. Eri stood near the edge of the plateau.

What was he doing here? Fool. He was going to get himself killed too. The artengo stopped its dive to glance over at the newcomer.

"Run, Eri!" Bas shouted.

The boy's face hardened like it often did when he was about to do something stupid, and not of the Urdahl. He ran for the closest crater.

"No!" Bas called.

The artengo looked between Bas and Eri. With Bas hurt, it decided Eri was the bigger threat and took off towards the boy.

Duat-damned fool!

Bas howled as he forced himself to his feet.

His leg screamed and he screamed with it. Another artengo noticed and flew at him. Pain consumed him. It dragged his focus to his leg. It burned and it shrieked. The bird drew closer.

And then silence.

Bas quietened everything.

The call of the birds.

The pain.

Even the night fell to blissful quiet.

The artengo opened its maw. Teeth like daggers dipped in red. Bas jammed his staff down the beast's throat. The artengo's eyes widened. It may have made a noise. Bas didn't know. Everything was silent. He then rammed the second half into the artengo's head. It fell to the stillness. He ripped out his staff, blood spraying across his face.

Bas panted as he looked at the edge of the platform then to Eri. Several artengo circled above the boy who was curled up in a nest. Bas had the beginnings of a plan to save Eri but it could mean the death of both of them. It was not Urdahl to save the boy. This was his choice. His mistake.

He silenced the thought.

Weightless and painless, Bas sprinted for Eri. There was no strain in his muscles. It felt more like floating than running.

Eri sat in the crater clutching an egg and shouting at the snapping artengo. Running to the edge, Bas threw himself at the bird hovering above the boy. His staff ends plunged into the artengo's back and together they crashed into the crater. The bird bucked and strained under Bas but it must have hit its head on the rock, its eyes rolling into its skull. Bas cut the beast's throat and watched as its blood began to pool in the crater.

Eri huddled in the corner holding an egg. Terror clear on his face.

Other artengo were flying above, cautious of Bas now that he had killed several of their kind. But that caution would only last so long.

"Eri, take an end of this glider," Bas said. He pulled the glider from his belt pocket and tried to hand an end to Eri who was staring at the twitching body of the artengo.

"You killed it." His mouth hung agape.

"Eri, I need you to focus." Bas grabbed the boy's head and forced him to meet his eyes. "Grab the end of the glider and stay here."

Eri nodded but Bas had to slide the end of the glider into his hand.

"Hold tight."

An artengo swooped for them. Just before it reached them, Bas side stepped and the artengo flew right into the glider's fabric. Bas leapt onto its back wrapping the glider around the beast. Panic seized the bird and it thrashed. Talons ripping through the fabric and tearing through Bas' way down from the high pass ridge. But the glider couldn't carry two anyway. It hadn't been an option.

They held the glider tight as the bird flailed. "Toss the egg," Bas said.

Eri glanced down as if he only just noticed that he was holding it.

"When we let go of the glider, the artengo will fly up and distract the others. You toss the egg in the opposite direction and we'll run for the edge of the plateau, okay?"

Eri nodded. He had gone pale.

"Now!"

They both released the glider and the artengo shot up in a tangle of fabric and feather. Bas yanked the boy's tunic to ensure he was following and then clambered out of the crater as Eri tossed the egg into the fray. Together, they sprinted through the nesting site. The artengo flew above, some snapping at the glider trying to free their friend and others chasing after the egg.

Bas came to the edge of the high ridge pass and slid off the cliff. It would be a long way down but with the glider in tatters they didn't have a choice. Eri eased onto the rock beside him.

They clambered down as fast as they could. The calls of the artengo a constant reminder that the beasts could fly after them at any moment.

"What were you thinking?" Bas asked.

"I… You didn't come back with the others. I thought you might be hurt," Eri said.

"So you came by yourself with no glider and no weapons?" Bas asked.

"I didn't think." Eri sounded like he was going to cry.

"You could have got us both killed!" Bas shouted. He reined in his tone. He was of the Urdahl. But he had never felt terror like he did the moment he saw Eri running for the egg. And it shook Bas to his core.

"I'm sorry," Eri said.

An artengo flew from the plateau above. It darted out looking for them. Bas sped up. The artengo circled and flew back towards the plateau.

"Stop," Bas said and they froze. The last light of the Moon Eye left little to see by. Perhaps—

The artengo cawed. It had spotted them. They were defenceless on the rock as it surged towards them.

"Eri, take the egg," Bas said. His mind a whirl.

"What?!" The boy knew the artengo would target whoever had the egg first. Bas tossed him the egg and Eri caught it in one hand.

Bas leapt up and then kicked off the cliff face.

Don't look down.

Just as the bird was about to snap at Eri, Bas landed on its back. The beast bucked and writhed.

"Jump!" Bas called.

Eri clung to the cliff, eyes wide but after a moment he jumped onto the artengo's back. Other artengo flew around them now. Bas stabbed into one of the bird's wings and they plummeted towards the black sand. Wind whistled. Bas focused on his breathing. They rocked back and forth as the artengo tried to fly upward but with its damaged wing it could do no more than slow their descent.

"Stay tight against it!" Bas said.

Bas brought his face deep into the artengo's feathers and closed his eyes. They crashed into the ground and went skidding across the dunes. Bas felt bones crack beneath him and the artengo went limp. They rolled and Bas scraped across the black sand.

They finally came to a stop, the wing of the artengo flopped over them, shielding them from the sky above where they heard the other birds shrieking.

Pain started to bleed back into Bas' leg. He closed his eyes and listened to his breathing.

Breathe in.

Breathe out.

Breathe in.

Breathe out.

Eventually, the call of the artengos drifted farther away until nothing but the steady breaths of Bas and Eri could be heard. Eri brushed aside the wing and gazed into the night.

"They're gone," Bas said, scanning the sky. He stood, groaning as he put weight on his wounded leg.

"Bas. I'm so sorry. I..." Eri's voice trailed off.

Bas was about to say it was okay. They had made it down alive and may yet return before first light. Then he noticed the ruptured egg in Eri's shaking hands. Goop poured through the cracks and onto the dunes. Tears brimmed in Eri's bloodshot eyes. His breath caught between a weep and a gasp.

Bas deflated, the strength draining from him like sand through a timer.

He had failed. The elder would not accept a cracked egg. A broken egg.

Bas couldn't help but see himself as the broken egg. Defective. Perhaps that was it, by some fate of the Gods one was born broken or whole and no matter what one did they could not change that. Like a broken egg, there was no putting the pieces back together.

He was no Urdahl.

He didn't say anything. He couldn't.

Instead, Bas turned and started walking back to the Settlement.

6

Of the Urdahl

"To be truly free, one must forsake that which they hold dear."
- Urdahl Proverb

First light illuminated Bas' failures and drowned him in overwhelming heat. He and Eri did not speak during their slow trudge back to the Settlement. It wasn't far and they might have made it before the Sun Eye began its watch. But what was the point? Bas had failed.

Wandering into the cavern, no one met them. Flames burned in braziers across the cavern walls but otherwise the entrance was empty. Revelry could be heard from deeper within the Settlement.

The Great Fire roared and the feast cavern was alight with more than flame. It was buzzing with conversation as Urdahl retold the tales of their testing. They ate artengo eggs and celebrated those who ascended to Urdahl.

Bas saw Mei at their usual spot with Rfan. Their eyes met and Mei nodded. There shouldn't be hard feelings between them. Bas should have foreseen her strategy. He should have been strong enough to stop anything that got in his way but he wasn't. It was Bas who had failed. But he did not nod back as he should have. He turned away and immediately felt petty, which made Bas feel worse.

Elder Niru walked between the fires. His face was hard and neutral. Some of his 700th year siblings were watching Bas but he didn't meet their gazes.

"Come," he said. "You too, Eri."

They followed the elder into his private quarters. The sitting room was an austere space with hard stone benches and a table on the far wall lined with bottles. The table had symbols carved into the wood, the only ornamentation Bas could see. Sweeping spirals swam up the legs of the table, ending with Ova's great Sun Eye and Moon Eye in the centre of the design. Pathways led deeper into his quarters where the elder slept and studied. Elder Niru gestured to the bench and Bas and Eri sat.

"Mei told me what happened," Elder Niru said.

"I was foolish not to anticipate her strategy," Bas said.

"This is true." Elder Niru filled two cups with a purple liquid. Then a third with a green liquid. He brought one of each over and handed the purple drink to Bas and the green to Eri. "You're too young to have any of this I'm afraid," Elder Niru said.

Eri nodded thanks and sipped the green drink.

"Mei told me that she had done thorough research into the cavern she dropped you in," Elder Niru said, picking up his cup. "It led back out to the high pass ridge. You should have had enough time to complete the testing even with the setback."

Bas glanced up. There were hundreds of caverns and tunnels mapped out and even more unmapped. How could she have known that the cavern would lead back out?

The book Mei had been reading the night before the testing. The Dark between the Light, Bas thought.

At the time he thought the title was unusual for a book about plants. That's because it was a book about tunnels. She had scoped out one that would allow him to find his way back to the high pass ridge and still complete the testing in time.

A surge of nausea swelled in his gut. Mei hadn't betrayed him. Not really. She had even tried to warn him by reminding him that it was a test of strength of mind as much as it was muscle. And he still failed.

"So then what was your failing?" Niru asked.

"I…" Bas' mind reeled.

"You are one of the best among your siblings. So then, why did they return before first light and you did not?"

Bas stammered out a half-formed word. He thought he had taken the blame onto himself but really in the back of his mind Bas had placed the blame on Mei.

"Is it because I am wrong in thinking you strong?"

"No, Elder Niru," Bas said.

"So then, Eri was the cause of your failure?" Elder Niru asked.

Eri choked on his drink and started coughing.

"There has been some concern that the boy is pulling you away from the Urdahl ways." Niru spoke as if Eri wasn't sitting beside him. "Your friendship has been noted by your siblings. You have given Eri special treatment and indulged his non-Urdahl tendencies."

"Elder, Eri needs extra help. He is Urdahl of heart. I want to help crave him into one of the best our people have to offer," Bas said, taken aback. But Bas could see the elder was trying to make sense of his failure.

"At what cost, Bas? You are one of the best of our people and now you have failed the testing. All the rules require me to label you as Unaged."

Eri continued to cough and splutter. Bas reserved the instinct to pat on the boy's back.

"But I can go to the other elders, tell them your testing was interrupted by Eri and place the blame on him," Elder Niru said. "Just tell me it was him who stopped you from completing the testing."

Was it Eri's fault?

If Mei had sent him to a tunnel that left him time to complete the testing then her betrayal wasn't the cause of his failure. Eri had broken the egg. With that, Bas had given up and walked slowly back to the Settlement. Could he have made it if Eri hadn't broken the egg?

He saved me.

Atop the plateau, if Eri hadn't called his name and distracted the artengo, Bas would have died.

Seeing Eri was a reminder of what Bas was fighting for

and gave him the strength to survive. It had brought him silence and a still mind when he needed it most. He fought for his brothers and sisters.

If Eri hadn't come Bas had no doubt in his mind that his corpse would be in one of those artengo nests putrefying in the Sun Eye's heat.

"Eri saved me. My failings are my own," Bas said. He felt the boy's gaze land on him but Bas kept his eyes on Elder Niru.

Niru stared at Bas for a moment and then sighed.

"I had hoped for more from you, Bas," Elder Niru said. "This softness for the boy is a problem. It seems I must cut off the corruption at the root."

Eri inhaled sharply. His face bloomed a deep red as he struggled to pull in air.

"Eri?" Bas asked.

"The tree is stronger from the loss of an infected branch," Elder Niru said.

A glaze covered Eri's once bright eyes. He hacked out a cough spraying blood across Bas' face as the mug that held the green liquid clattered to the floor.

"You are one of the best among us, Bas, and you will thank me for this in years to come," Elder Niru said.

Cold swept through Bas as Eri fell against him. His skin burned to the touch. Eyes wide and panicked.

"Eri? What's wrong?" Bas' thoughts refused to catch up with the situation.

Eri floundered, sputtering and clutching his throat. Bas smacked the boy's back trying to free whatever had stuck.

Eri thrashed.

Bas didn't understand.

Eri stilled. Face frozen in a rictus of terror. Veins bulged on the boy's forehead as his body strained for air until the last gasp. Bas reached out with trembling fingers and felt for Eri's pulse.

There was none.

Bas had trained his entire life to survive pain. But the pain of loss, the silence, the stillness. There was no preparing for that.

One cannot prepare for the breaking off of part of one's soul.

"How did you learn of it? I will have to snap back at any

leaks, of course," Elder Niru.

Bas looked up. His mind was too muddled to attempt to piece together the elders' words.

Elder Niru raised an eyebrow. "You didn't know he was your blood brother?"

Shock ran through Bas.

Blood brother?

Eri had been his blood brother? The Urdahl never let one know of their parentage or true blood siblings. The elders said it led to weakness.

Bas glanced down. The stink of death already poured off Eri and his face had gone purple. Bas wiped some of the blood from his face. His brother's blood.

"There is strength in blood," Elder Niru muttered. He looked between Bas and Eri as if they were a quandary to ponder.

Had fate tied them together because Bas was supposed to care for his brother? Had he failed at that too? Or was it by chance? Somehow, that was worse.

"Do not fear, Bas," Elder Niru said, his usually hard voice was soft. Niru pulled Eri's body from the bench and let it thud onto the ground, discarded. "You're free now. I would kill a thousand Eri's for one such as yourself. I will tell the other elders that Eri interrupted your testing." He sat beside Bas and laid a hand on his shoulder.

Bas couldn't take his eyes off of Eri's corpse. His blood-shot eyes stared into Bas.

"You're of the Urdahl, Bas," Niru said. "You're one of us."

Bas wallowed in the space between emotions. He took his place among his 700th year siblings as an Urdahl and no one mentioned the testing. No one mentioned Eri. Not one of Eri's year siblings asked about his whereabouts. It was as if he never existed.

With the turning season coming to a close, the Settlement fell into routine. Urdahl bustled about training and medi-tating. No one else seemed to notice the quiet where once there was noise. No one else seemed to notice an Urdahl less wandering the wind tunnels. No one else seemed to notice the empty bed in the 712th sibling's chamber.

But Bas noticed.

His nights were plagued with the oncoming darkness. It

spread through the tunnels and caverns of the Settlement. Eri's shouts for help echoed through the black but Bas could never find him. And eventually, his calls fell silent.

Every night was the same and the days were little better.

The Sun Eye brought no heat atop his meditation perch. The endless desert sprawling out in front of him seemed empty. Bas reached into his cloak and pulled out a book. Eri's book. He flicked through to the point he left off and started reading.

The hero and his party faced the demon. They fought hard but it was clear they couldn't win. So the hero sacrificed himself to let his friends get away.

That was how the story ended. In blood and death. The darkness hadn't been banished. The hero's sister had been saved but at what cost? The hero was dead and the sister would have to live with that. Live with the guilt that it was for her that he died. He traded his life for hers and she hadn't asked for such a heavy burden.

Flashes of Eri's purple terror-stricken face haunted the recesses in Bas' mind. He had saved Bas twice.

Did Eri know he was a hero when he died? Bas hoped so.

Bas felt tears streak his face. A weakness. One he allowed the Sun Eye to burn away.

Was he to continue on like nothing happened? Was he to hide the pain and take up his place as a fully-fledged Urdahl?

Bas didn't know what that meant anymore.

He glanced at the book in his lap. When he started the book, Bas had thought that it followed characters who tried to create a world without pain. But that wasn't true. The characters had known it would end in blood and tears. And yet they quested out to try anyway. A foolish impossible pursuit.

The hero had failed. He had died but it was never about succeeding. It was about following the dream. It was about living and pushing through the pain in an attempt to create a better world. In that way, this piece of fiction held more knowledge into the Urdahl ideals than some of their scholarly texts.

Being Urdahl was more than surviving pain. It was living. It was following the foolish pursuits. For it is better to fall fighting the demon, than it is to live under its reign.

Bas closed the book.

He made his way through the wind tunnels to the Wayup cavern.

Sunlight poured into the cave as Bas walked along the wall until he came across the scuffs of boot prints. It didn't take him long to find the nook that Eri liked to read in. Bas clambered into it. It was tight but he could see why Eri liked it here. He could look out onto the desert from this height but he could also see into the Settlement. A threshold between two worlds.

Something jabbed into his thigh. Bas reached under himself and pulled out a book. He shook his head. If the elders knew Eri had smuggled more than one book out of the temple he would have got a lashing.

He opened the cover. The title read, *"Voice of the Hero: Book 2."*

It was the sequel to *Voice of the People*. Bas flicked through the first couple pages. A revenge tale of a sister taking on the evil that stole her brother.

Tendrils of fate tugged at Bas. He wouldn't let Eri's sacrifice be in vain. Bas looked out at Yontar on the horizon.

Elder Niru was wrong. Taking Eri away had weakened Bas, not made him stronger. He felt the hollowness where a fire once roared.

He should let the darkness flood this place. The vision promised blood and Bas would bathe in it.

Eri's voice came unbidden, echoing through that darkness. *Pain is inevitable but that inevitability is not a right to inflict it upon others.*

This wasn't what Eri would have wanted. If he let the vision come to pass, he would be allowing the pain to consume him and infect those around him. Even those who meant him no harm like his brothers and sisters. He had to be strong like Eri.

Bas' grip tightened around the book. He would stop the oncoming darkness and he would save the Settlement and his siblings. Or he would die trying.

Eri was the hero but Bas would see what he could do.

For he was of the Urdahl and he would show them all.

ACKNOWLEDGMENTS

While writing *Harbinger of Justice*, Bas' story was developing in the back of my mind. Where had this quiet man come from? Who were these Urdahl? And so, as I prepared to work on the sequel, *The Black Mantle*, I knew I had to delve into his origins and this unique sub-culture in Tarris first. But like any book, the name on the cover does little to convey the amount of people that helped bring this story to life.

Firstly, I want to thank Zack and Hillary Argyle for all they do for the indie book community. Being selected as a winner of the Indie Fantasy Fund in 2023 was an honour and a huge help in offsetting some of the publishing costs.

My beta reader team whose early comments strengthened the story. And my ARC reader team who shared their experience with all who would listen.

My patrons who help fund these books. Including high tier patrons; Brett, Karl, Marija, and Scott.

My cover artist, Chris Nazgul, who did a terrific job capturing Bas and the Tarrisian landscape.

My editor, Sarah Chorn, who not only makes my writing readable but makes me a better writer too.

My family for their continued support. From being my first readers to just wanting the pretty covers, I couldn't do it without you all.

And lastly, the readers. Without readers, stories are nothing but mad ramblings. It's the reader who imagines the world and characters and make them real.

So thank you for making my story real.

ABOUT THE AUTHOR

Andrew Watson lives on the outskirts of Edinburgh where he rambles about made up people and places. He has a first class degree in Digital Media from Edinburgh Napier University and currently works as a freelance video editor and author. Andrew can also be found on YouTube and Instagram where he jumps around excitedly shouting about books.

Follow Andrew at:
andrew-watson.co.uk
@the_fools_tale

www.ingramcontent.com/pod-product-compliance
Lightning Source LLC
Chambersburg PA
CBHW021723190726

48289CB00008B/2673